WAY OUT WEST ON MY LITTLE PONY

WAY OUT WEST ON MY LITTLE PONY

By Jan Peck

Illustrated by Herb Leonhard

PELICAN PUBLISHING COMPANY

GRETNA 2010

The word "Pelican" and the depiction of a pelican
are trademarks of Pelican Publishing Company, Inc.,
and are registered in the U.S. Patent and Trademark Office.

Library of Congress Cataloging-in-Publication Data

Peck, Jan.
  Way out west on my little pony / by Jan Peck ; illustrated by Herb Leonhard.
      p. cm.
  Summary: A child encounters many critters while riding down the trail on a pony.
  ISBN 978-1-58980-697-9 (alk. paper)
  [1. Stories in rhyme. 2. Ponies--Fiction. 3. Animals--Fiction. 4. West (U.S.)--Fiction.] I. Leonhard,
Herb, ill. II. Title.
  PZ8.3.P2754Waz 2010
  [E]--dc22
                          2009030283

Printed in Singapore
Published by Pelican Publishing Company, Inc.
1000 Burmaster Street, Gretna, Louisiana 70053

WAY OUT WEST ON MY LITTLE PONY

Way out West on my little pony,
I'm riding down the trail
to see what I can see.
I'm so brave,
can't scare me,
way out West on my little pony.

Way out West on my little pony,
I find a horned toad wiggling by me.
Howdy, horned toad.
Freckled belly,
horned toad.

See you later, horned toad.
Trot away.

Way out West on my little pony,
I find a prairie dog barking at me.

Howdy, prairie dog.
Stand tall, prairie dog.
See you later, prairie dog.
Trot away.

Way out West on my little pony,
I find an armadillo digging by me.
Howdy, armadillo.
Jump up, armadillo.
See you later, armadillo.
Trot away.

Way out West on my little pony,
I find a raccoon washing by me.
Howdy, raccoon.

Scrub-a-dub, raccoon.
See you later, raccoon.
Trot away.

Way out West on my little pony,
I find a jackrabbit hopping by me.
Howdy, jackrabbit.

All ears, jackrabbit.
See you later, jackrabbit.
Trot away.

Way out West on my little pony,
I find a roadrunner racing by me.
Howdy, roadrunner.
Shake a leg, roadrunner.

See you later, roadrunner.
Trot away.

Way out West on my little pony,
I find a striped skunk stinking by me.

Howdy, skunk.
Smelly tail-y, skunk!
See you later, skunk.
Trot away.

Way out West on my little pony,
I find a coyote howling at me.
Howdy, coyote.
High note, coyote.
See you later, coyote.
Trot away.

Way out West on my little pony,
I find a buffalo charging by me.
Howdy, buffalo.

What a show, buffalo!
See you later, buffalo.
Trot away.

Way out West on my little pony,
I find a longhorn snorting by me.

Howdy, longhorn.
Rootin' tootin', longhorn.
See you later, longhorn.
Trot away.

Way out West on my little pony,
I find a rattler shaking at me!

So long, rattlesnake!
So long, longhorn.
So long, buffalo.
So long, coyote.
So long, stinky skunk.
So long, roadrunner.
So long, jackrabbit.
So long, raccoon.
So long, armadillo.
So long, prairie dog.
So long, horned toad.

Way back home on my little pony,
I find Grandpa waiting for me.
Howdy, Grandpa!
Guess what, Grandpa?

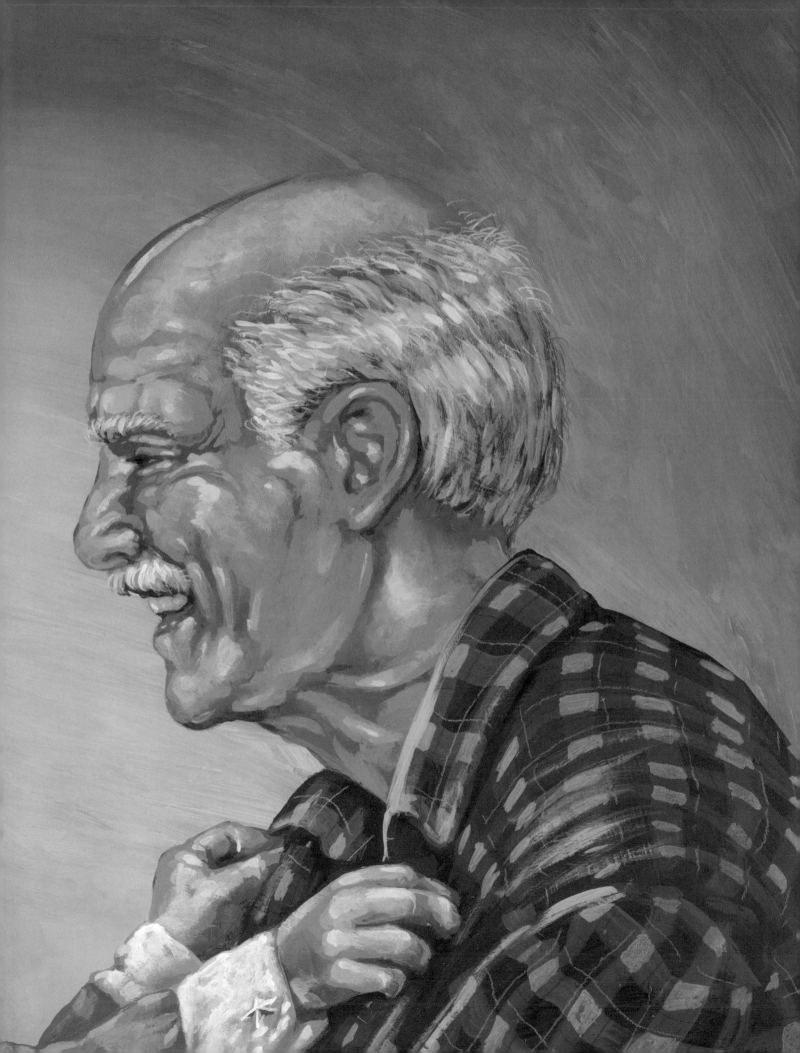

I rode out West on my little pony!